SWEET TREATS AND DIRTY DEEDS

DOG DETECTIVE - THE BEAGLE MYSTERIES

ROSIE SAMS

AGATHA PARKER

SWEETBOOKHUB.COM

* * *

THE DOG DETECTIVES – THE BEAGLE MYSTERIES

Welcome to my book. I recently joined forces with the amazing Rosie Sams to work on this wonderful series of cozy mystery books all featuring a sweet little Beagle puppy. Mazie is an ex-police dog who was wounded in service. She is gifted to Hannah Barry, a broken-hearted realtor who is down on her luck.

At first, Hannah is unsure, can she learn to love the Beagle? What will she do when a body is found?

Find out how Mazie found a new home and Hannah some peace in book one of this series Sniffing out the killer each book can be read alone.

Rosie has a free book Smudge and the Stolen Puppies that you can pick up. It is about an amazing and cute

French Bulldog the best Dog Detective in all of Port Warren. Grab it here for FREE

CHAPTER ONE

Hannah Barry looked up at the stars and breathed in a deep breath. The air was cool and refreshing but she felt good. It was a brisk November evening, and she sat with friends on the heated patio of the hottest new restaurant in town, Troughton's Trough. What could be better?

Hannah had recently traded in her job as a local realtor and become a private investigator. Tonight, she was sharing a meal with her friend, Colin Troughton, the restaurant owner, and her trusted beagle, Mazie. The ex-police dog had landed in Hannah's lap just a few months ago. Though she had been reluctant to take on a dog, Mazie's keen sense of smell and police training had come in handy. The dog's company even more so and she had to admit that she was smitten with the little bundle of fun. Though she had been shot on duty, Mazie rarely limped and lived her life to the full, especially when it came to finding treats. The little pup was giving Colin her soulful eyes even now and it worked. Colin artfully slipped her a piece of the delicious cheese bread beneath the table. Hannah wished she could eat as much and stay so trim.

Tonight, the trio were savoring the delightful food in celebration of Hannah's successful first case.

Blairstown. Vermont, was a quaint, small town, but not small enough to avoid crime. Hannah seemed to have a knack for finding herself at the center of solving them, so much so that she decided to formally go into business. Now an official P.I., she was off to a running start. With the help of both Colin and Mazie, she had solved the murder of a local businessman. In doing so, she'd helped release two other people from prison who had been falsely accused of the crime.

While they were eating. two of Hannah's friends, Oscar and Anita Gomez, happened to walk by and decided to join them for dinner. Hannah couldn't help but notice that they weren't their usual happy selves. "What is it?" she asked.

"We think we may need your help," Anita said.

"Some of your P.I. help," Oscar added.

Hannah felt her eyes open wide and Mazie gave a little bark. Though it could have been demanding more food rather than offering her own help.

"Go on," Hannah said.

"With one of our former employees." Anita let out a sigh that made her look exhausted.

Hannah didn't hesitate and jumped at the chance to help two of her best friends. "What can I do?"

Anita and Oscar exchanged a glance. Anita squirmed in her seat and cast her eyes to the table.

"I need to know exactly what's going on if I'm to help you properly," Hannah said gently. "I'm all ears and it is fully confidential." She folded her arms on the table and leaned toward her friends.

Oscar squeezed Anita's hand and gave her a slight nod. "One of our former employees, Chris Welsh," she paused to narrow her eyes at Hannah, "do you remember him?"

Hannah nodded. She and Mazie spent so much time at the Gómezes coffee shop, Jolt of Java, that she felt she knew most of their employees. "Isn't he the younger one who had shaggy, light brown hair?" she asked.

"That's him," Anita confirmed. "One day he came into the store and just quit. No notice or anything. It was so strange to us because we had just met with him to discuss putting him on the manager track and he seemed so happy about it."

Hannah nodded. "What does this have to do with Chris?"

"We think that when Chris left Jolt of Java, he took some of our recipes with him." Anita's eyes hardened at this confession.

"I hope it wasn't the croissant recipe," Colin said. "You have the best in town, even Mazie thinks so!" He looked down at the beagle. A croissant from Anita and Oscar was one of her favorite treats.

"Our croissants, and then some," Oscar said. "We think he's selling the recipes to rival coffee shops across town, and it's started cutting into our profits."

Hannah listened carefully. "Do you have any proof that he did this? Security footage, eyewitnesses, even a hot tip from someone?"

Anita shook her head mournfully. "We don't have any proof. We didn't suspect a thing when he was with us as he was a model employee. We had no reason to imagine anyone who worked for us would want to do something like this."

"But we have seen our pastries, yes, croissants included, popping up all over town," Oscar said. "Our specialty cinnamon swirl bread, the recipe which was handed down from my abuela, showed up suddenly at Peter's Coffee Shop. We even went to taste it to confirm our suspicions. It's an exact replica." Oscar had a fire in his eyes. "Why would he do such a thing?"

"Did anyone else have access to these recipes?" Hannah asked.

Oscar and Anita both shook their heads. "No one," he said. "We take it all very seriously and keep the recipes locked in a safe. He was the only other person who knew the code. Anita and I try to do all the baking for our place because we can never be too careful."

"Or so we thought," Anita added.

"I have seen Chris wearing an apron, though," Hannah said.

"Yes," Oscar agreed. "He did work in the kitchen occasionally. And a few times when we were sick or on vacation, Chris did actually reference the recipes and bake for us. I guess that's when he must have stolen them."

"I'm so sorry this is happening to you both," Hannah said.

Oscar looked meaningfully at Hannah. "Would you consider digging around to try and find proof that Chris is our culprit?" he asked her. "With no proof, we can't do anything. We are losing money each week and can no longer claim that these are exclusive products!"

"We just want to take appropriate legal action," Anita added. "We just want to stop people using these recipes however we can."

Hannah looked across the table at Anita and Oscar, taking in their worried frowns. She hated to see how distraught they were and wanted to help in any way she could. "Of course, I'll help you. I won't stop until I find out who took your recipes. And I'll start with Chris Welsh," she vowed.

It was as if Mazie could sense the shift in Hannah's tone. The little beagle turned away from Colin and stood on her hind legs to put her paws on Hannah's lap. Colin patted Mazie's head. "I'm with you both. I'll do anything I can to help Hannah with her investigation," he said.

Anita squeezed Oscar's hand. "We can't thank you enough, Hannah," Oscar said, gratitude oozing from him.

"We feel bad that we are giving you another case during your celebration dinner for completing your previous one," Anita said.

"You know me, I love a mystery and it's the least I can do for you both. Turning to Colin she winked. "Raincheck on dessert?"

He nodded. Hannah picked up her purse and Colin stood too.

"Let's go track down Chris?" he said.

CHAPTER TWO

Hannah, Colin, and Mazie said goodbye to Anita and Oscar. "You go get some rest," Colin said. "Your case is in good hands with Hannah here." He smiled and patted Hannah on her shoulder.

Hannah warmed at both his compliment and his touch and clipped Mazie's leash on her harness.

Anita scribbled Chris's address down on a slip of paper, sliding it into Hannah's hand. "Thanks again," she whispered.

Hannah looked at the address. "He lives all the way across town, I guess we should take a car," she said to Colin. Blairstown was set up so you could walk almost anywhere if you had the time. But given the late hour and the cold weather, they agreed that driving would be best.

About ten minutes later, they pulled into a parking spot in front of a condo. Hannah and Colin exchanged a quick glance as they approached the front door. She rang the bell and waited. Chris was there to greet them in no time. He swung the door open and they were met with a look of surprise on his face.

"Chris, hello," Hannah said.

Chris furrowed his brow and ran a hand through his hair as if buying time to place where he may have seen her before.

Hannah helped him out. "My name is Hannah Barry, and I'm a friend of Oscar and Anita Gomez," she said, reaching out her hand for him to shake.

Something seemed to click for him suddenly, and he reached his hand to meet Hannah's. "Of course! I'm sorry, that took me a minute. You know how it is when you see someone out of context," he said. "It's quite a surprise to see you here, I must say."

"We're sorry to drop by unannounced like this," she said. "This is my friend, Colin," she gestured to her tall friend. "And this is my dog, Mazie." At the mention of her name, Mazie's tail wagged enthusiastically.

Chris looked at Mazie and couldn't help but smile. He widened the door. "Would you like to come in?" he asked. "I'm sure I have something to offer you." He backed away from the threshold of his condo, gesturing for them to follow him inside.

Hannah looked at Colin and raised her eyebrows. He shrugged in return and the two of them joined Chris at his kitchen table. On her way there, Hannah glanced around his living space and took in the details. Hardly any surface area was left uncovered, whether by books, articles of clothing, bills, or other random household objects. To say the small space was cluttered was an understatement. But Chris didn't seem to notice or mind. Unlike most people, he didn't point out the clutter.

When they sat at the table, a woman with a rich shade of dyed red hair, wearing sweatpants and a t-shirt walked down the stairs. "Who have we here?" she asked Chris, folding her arms across her chest, her right hip jutted out as if she was posing.

Chris hardly glanced in her direction. "Hey, babe, this is Hannah, Colin, and Mazie," he said. When he set a glass of water in front of each of them. "This is Emma Porter. My girlfriend."

Hannah and Colin looked at Emma and said hello. Emma didn't respond but came to sit at the table, arms still folded as she slumped into a chair across from them with a face like a wet weekend.

Chris sat next to her. "So, what brings you to our home this evening?"

Hannah got right to the point. "Anita and Oscar have suspicions that their recipes are being sold all over town," she watched carefully to gauge Chris's reaction. His face was expressionless.

"They claim that you were the only other one with access to the recipes. I'm here to ask you plainly if you took them and sold them to other coffee shops." Sometimes Hannah felt the need to tread lightly in conversations such as these. This time, she felt Chris would respect a direct approach and that she would gain more from his reaction rather than warning him by beating about the bush.

Chris straightened in his seat, while Emma stayed quiet in hers. Her lips pursed and her arms crossed slightly tighter than before.

"That's an interesting question," Chris replied. "Especially given the fact that I was at Jolt of Java every day at 4 A.M., baking for the store. I would come in on weekends to experiment with recipes. Sometimes scrapping an entire batch of something to try again with just a teaspoon variation in the recipe." He seemed very passionate about his position.

Hannah looked from Chris to Emma, but she was still silent. That was part of her training as a P.I. If you kept quiet people felt a need to fill the silence.

Chris continued. "Considering I am the brains behind the pastry operation, and I'm the one that created and tweaked those recipes until they were perfect, you'd think that I have every right to sell them to the highest bidder." He stopped to stare hard at Hannah. "Would you agree?" he asked her pointedly.

There was no doubt that Chris was convincing, and under other circumstances, Hannah might even have believed him. But if she knew anything, it was that Oscar and Anita Gomez were trustworthy, and would never have come to her unless they were in a huge jam. She looked at Chris to reply. "In theory, Chris, I would agree. But I can't help but wonder if you are being entirely truthful, if this is a simple case of miscommunication, or – and this is more probable to me – if you are just trying to spin a quick profit?" she said.

Chris didn't say anything in response. He didn't have to, because his face spoke for him. It had turned the color of slate.

Emma noticed as well and took it as her opportunity to finally speak up. She scooted her chair out from the table, stood, and walked directly up to Hannah. She pointed a finger in her face. "You, Ms. Barry, are in league with Oscar and Anita. I don't know what exactly they told you but it's a lie. And it seems like you've been sent to do their dirty work," she said.

Emma had moved so close to her that Hannah could feel the spittle from her words. Hannah had never been in a fight before, but she was worried that her record was about to change.

Mazie, who was never far from Hannah, sensed the tension and began barking frantically. She circled Emma's feet, each bark seeming to get louder. The noise took Emma by surprise, and she stepped away from Hannah.

Hannah was grateful to Mazie for the distraction and managed to reach down and loop her finger under Mazie's collar and shuffle the dog over to Colin's care.

Then she boldly turned back to Chris, who was still sitting at the table. "If the recipes are, in fact, yours – why didn't you go through the proper legal channels to prove it?"

Chris had no answer and simply shrugged in response. Emma came quickly to his defense and moved close to Hannah again. She jabbed her index finger in Hannah's chest. "It's time for you and your friends to be leaving now," she said angrily.

Hannah had to agree. She couldn't find a way to change the unexpected tone of the evening, so was happy to find her way back through the clutter to the front door. Once she, Colin, and Mazie were outside, they made their way back to Colin's car.

Colin, who had accompanied Hannah on a few of these investigations at this point, could sense that Hannah was about to ruminate out loud about what she had just seen, so he wisely stayed quiet. Sure enough, as soon as the doors to the car were closed, Hannah spoke. "Something doesn't feel right about what just happened."

Colin turned on the engine to warm up the car. "Which part?" he asked. "When Emma almost tried to fight you twice, or when Chris lied?"

Hannah turned to look into his green eyes. "All of it together. I just feel there is much more to this story than meets the eye," she said. Then she reached to slip Mazie a treat in the back seat. "And I intend to get to the bottom of it," she said, resolutely looking out the windshield.

Colin smiled to himself. "I expected nothing less," he said and drove them back to Hannah's house.

CHAPTER THREE

Once they were back on Hannah's side of town, Colin parked the car at her place. Instead of going into her house, Hannah turned to Colin. "What do you say we go for some dessert?" she asked, a twinkle in her eye.

Mazie seemed to recognize the word and began barking.

Colin laughed. "I'm always up for dessert," he said. "But let me guess, there's more to it than a little sugar craving?"

Hannah smiled. "Well, aren't you insightful? But you're right. I want to check out one of the spots that Anita and Oscar said were using their recipes," she said.

"Great idea, did you have a specific place in mind?"

"I was thinking we should start with Cody's Café. It's got on-site dining, and they sell desserts exclusively," she said.

"Sounds like a plan to me," Colin replied.

Hannah hooked Mazie's leash on her harness and the three of them walked toward Cody's Café. Only a few blocks later, they found themselves standing in front of the romantic restaurant. "Maybe I'll get some ideas for Troughton's Trough," Colin joked to Hannah.

Hannah rolled her eyes. "Just what we need, another pastry thief in town!" she said.

Colin held the door for Hannah and Mazie to walk through. "Welcome!" a plump woman wearing an apron called to them. "Take a seat wherever you'd like. There's a spot by the window that looks great for you two love-birds," she said.

"Oh, we aren't together," Hannah quickly corrected the woman.

The woman winked at Hannah, her rosy cheeks filling her face. "Yet."

Hannah, a little flustered, rushed to the empty table by the window. Mazie trotted behind her. Colin sat across from her, an amused grin plastered on his face. Hannah opened the menu, deliberately avoiding his eyes.

"What looks good to you?" Colin asked Hannah and as she looked up he winked.

Feeling her insides melt like a chocolate pudding Hannah dropped her eyes to the menu. "I was thinking about the chocolate cake."

"Same here, that looks delicious. Should we split it?" Colin asked.

The blush crept further up Hannah's collar. "Great idea," she said, folding the menu.

The woman in the apron came to their table, notebook in hand. "My name is Lucille Cody. I'll be helping you out tonight. What's it going to be for you both?" she asked.

"I think we'll split the chocolate cake," Hannah replied.

"One cake, two forks, coming right up!" she beamed. Just as she turned to walk away, Hannah placed her hand on Lucille's arm.

"Excuse me, Lucille?" she asked.

"Did you forget something?"

"Not exactly, we wanted to ask you about a man named Chris Welsh. Do you know him?" Hannah asked.

Lucille didn't miss a beat. "Of course, I know Chris. He came in here asking if I needed any new recipes. He mentioned something about how we needed to refresh our menu to keep customers happy, and then he showed me a whole book of ideas."

Hannah was impressed. Chris's operation was more sophisticated than she pictured it would be. "And did you buy any of the recipes?"

"Oh, yes. He not only had a book, but he came with samples. I made sure to try every single offering he had, and finally chose three of my favorites," she replied.

"How are the new recipes selling?" Hannah asked.

Lucille looked delighted. "They are some of our best sellers!" she replied. "Chris was a little non-conventional. Some might even call him suspicious, but I paid him for the recipes and haven't regretted it since.

Hannah glanced at Colin and raised her eyebrows. Lucille caught the exchange and asked, "Am I missing something here? Is there anything you need to tell me?"

Hannah sighed. "We're investigating a claim that Chris stole recipes and sold them to local stores."

Lucille gasped and clutched her hands to her chest. "I would never steal a recipe!" she said.

"No, no," Hannah said quickly. "We don't mean you. We mean Chris."

Realization set in and Lucille crumpled. "Ah, I see." She looked between Colin and Hannah. "His prices were pretty low for the quality of those recipes. I guess I should have known it was too good to be true," she said. "I'm so sorry about the mix-up. I would never knowingly use stolen recipes, and I want you to know I will stop production of the recipes immediately."

Hannah was impressed with Lucille's stance. "That's very kind of you, Lucille, we appreciate it. I'll tell the original owners that you have three of their recipes; they will be so grateful to you."

Lucille sighed. "Part of the business, I'm afraid. But thanks for stopping by. And here's a little something for the puppy," she said, tossing a piece of bread to Mazie. Mazie gobbled it up in seconds. "Is that the honey-sweet potato bread?" Hannah asked.

"Wow, great eye. It is indeed. That's one of Chris' recipes," Lucille said, looking at the floor. "We'll be sad to say goodbye to those recipes, but it's the right thing to do."

Hannah and Colin stood to leave, while Mazie sniffed Lucille's feet, hoping for more bread. Once they were out of the café, Colin turned to Hannah. "So, no chocolate cake, then?"

Hannah laughed. "I guess not, we must have shocked her with the bomb about the stolen recipes. But there is some good news," she said.

"What's that?"

"Dornan's Desserts is next," Hannah said. "We can get dessert there."

"You're on." Colin took her arm as they walked one block down the city center to the next location.

When they arrived at a storefront with a navy-blue awning, they knew they were at Dornan's Desserts. Colin checked his watch. "They close in five minutes."

"Well then, just enough time to slip in there and grab something sweet," Hannah replied.

The tinkle of the bell alerted Burke Dornan to their arrival. The bald man eyed them when they walked in. "We're closed," he said in a gruff voice from behind the counter.

"We just wanted to grab a quick pastry to go. Do you have any honey-sweet potato bread?" Hannah asked.

"And chocolate cake?" Colin added.

Burke wordlessly slid the glass door of the pastry case open and pulled out their two requests. With a frown, he packaged the items up. Colin smiled, never taking his eyes off the chocolate cake.

"I just love that bread," Hannah said. "Have you been making it a long time? I find it's not a flavor that many people carry." She quickly glanced at Colin to see if he'd notice her approach, but he was focused on the cake.

"It's a new recipe," Burke said.

"Oh! Did you get it from Chris Welsh?" she asked.

Burke's eyes flashed up at her and he stopped wrapping the items. Colin looked at Hannah, panicked. "What makes you ask that?" Burke asked.

"I've just heard that he sold a few recipes to some local store owners. And that they were pretty inexpensive. Did you find that suspicious?" she asked.

"I paid good money for these recipes," he replied. "And I don't appreciate you or anyone else coming into my store to suggest otherwise."

"Mr. Dornan, I'm not suggesting anything of the sort. I've been asked to investigate because a few recipes have been stolen from Jolt of Java, and we've got a lead on Chris Welsh so, I was just following up."

"Jolt of Java, huh?" Burke went back to packaging the pastries, and Colin's shoulders relaxed. "Oscar and Anita might be the ones you should be speaking with. The two of them took advantage of Chris for a long time, before he got wise to their – how should I phrase this – illicit activities. It sounds to me like they are trying to put the attention on someone else, so they aren't found out."

Hannah bristled at the suggestion that her friends had done anything wrong. "Mr. Burke, with all due respect, I know Oscar and Anita very well. They are involved in no such thing."

Burke put the pastries on top of the glass counter and stepped out from behind it, walking dangerously close to Hannah. His imposing stature towered over her.

Mazie began growling and positioned herself at her owner's feet. The noise was low in her throat but all the more menacing for it.

Colin finally took his eyes off of the chocolate cake and stepped between Hannah and Burke. "Watch yourself, Burke. Threatening a lady is not going to end well for you."

Burke's eyebrows shot up. "Is that a threat? I'm going to call my lawyer if I see either of you in my store again. You all need to leave, now!"

Colin placed his hand on Hannah's lower back and gently nudged her to the door, careful to keep between her and Burke.

Once they were outside, Hannah turned to Colin, breathless. "Thank you so much for sticking up for me in there. I could never have predicted his reaction." She placed her hand on her chest to try and settle her racing heart. "I still think Chris is dirty, but I need more proof he actually stole the recipes."

Colin agreed. "Chris does seem to be dirty dealing, but I thought what Burke said about Oscar and Anita was pretty interesting," he added carefully.

Hannah felt her blood start to boil. Yes, the man had just saved her but... "Oscar and Anita? How could you take anything that angry man said seriously? He was obviously trying to throw a flare to keep us off his case," she said.

"I'm just taking into consideration all the factors, and trying to keep emotion and relationship out of it," he said.

Hannah exhaled, knowing she couldn't disregard anything at this point. "Let's put a pin in it until we gain more information," she said.

"Agreed." He looked around at the closed shops and empty streets. "By the way, do you know any place I can get a slice of chocolate cake? I've got a real craving for it now."

Hannah couldn't help but laugh as they headed toward her office.

CHAPTER FOUR

Hannah unlocked her office door and Mazie ran directly to her doggy bed in the corner. Hannah threw her a chew to keep her occupied while she sat at her desk to go through her notes so far.

"Are you sure you don't want to go home and get some sleep? We can start back up in the morning." Colin asked.

"I'm on a roll now, I want to keep the momentum going while I have it all at the top of mind."

"Suit yourself," he said, stretching out to lay on the couch in her office. Hannah busied herself typing her notes and working through some files on her computer. She wanted to run a background report on Chris. She typed in her password and pressed enter. Tapping her fingers on the desk, she waited while the background report was processed. The digital circle in the center of her screen glowed as she waited for it to populate a PDF. As she waited, she was interrupted by the sound of snoring. She turned to see Colin fast asleep on the couch behind her. She glanced at Mazie in her dog bed, who was peacefully resting her chin on her chew, her eyes closed. She smiled and turned back to her computer. The report had populated; Hannah eagerly leaned toward her screen to see what she would learn.

She covered her mouth with her hand as she read through the information. Chris had switched jobs multiple times in the past few years. All at various restaurants as a cook. "Hmm, interesting," she mumbled, chewing on a pen.

She typed his name in the internet search engine along with one of the listed restaurants and up popped a news report. His girlfriend, Emma, had owned one of the establishments he worked in but had to file for bankruptcy recently when she ran it into the ground. "Very interesting," Hannah said, out loud this time.

Colin roused from the couch at her voice. He sat up abruptly and looked around as if surprised. "Interesting? What's interesting?" he asked.

Hannah turned to Colin, laughing at his disheveled hair and dazed look. "I just found out something interesting about Chris *and* Emma," she said. "Emma used to own a restaurant, she hired Chris, and now she's filed for bankruptcy because the restaurant went under."

Colin ran his hand over his face as if to clear the fog. "That does sound suspicious. On many levels."

"I wonder if Chris might be a pawn here. Maybe Emma is the one who needs the cash, and she convinced Chris to steal and sell the recipes to pay off her debt." Hannah shrugged.

Colin nodded. "That sounds reasonable to me. I think you may be on the right track here. What do you say we go talk to Oscar and Anita again to run it by them? Maybe they knew something about Emma or even met her while Chris worked for them. It'd be interesting to hear their insight about her."

"Great idea." Hannah looked at a sleepy Colin, then at a sleeping Mazie, and yawned herself. "But why don't we do that tomorrow? It's been a very long day, and I could use a good night's sleep," she said.

Colin's grin lit up his whole face. "I thought you'd never ask!" he said. "I'll drive you and Mazie home and pick you up again in the morning. I've got a plush, King-sized bed waiting for me to fall fast asleep in," he said. "Just a shame there's no chocolate cake."

Hannah gathered her notes and purse and scooped Mazie up into her arms. "Deal. I will treat you to chocolate cake when the case is over."

Colin's face broke into a huge smile.

* * *

THE NEXT MORNING, Colin parked in front of Hannah's house at 9:00 A.M. She peeked through her blinds, ready to go, and ran down her front porch carrying Mazie. She was in Colin's passenger seat and buckled before he had turned his engine off to ring her doorbell.

"Morning," she said, catching her jagged breath from her short sprint to the car. "Ready for some coffee?"

Colin smiled and reversed the car. "Jolt of Java, here we come."

They drove carefully through the lingering morning fog toward the Gómezes coffee shop. When they pulled up to the store, they saw Oscar outside, arguing with someone who had their back to them. Hannah squinted her eyes. "Does that look like Chris to you?"

Colin studied the man. "It could be. There's only one way to find out," he said, unbuckling his seat belt.

Hannah clipped Mazie's leash to her harness and they walked toward the two gentlemen. She heard the angry voices as she neared the men. Oscar moved a step closer to Chris and raised his voice so she could hear him. "You'll be sorry if you keep coming around this shop. Leave. Now!" he said, pointing his finger next to Chris's face."

Anita rushed over and grabbed Oscar's arm, pulling him away to a corner.

Colin approached Chris and slipped a casual arm around him. "Hey, man. Why don't we step away for a few minutes?" Chris seemed to calm slightly under Colin's touch.

Hannah noticed Oscar's face was still red, and his body was still stiff, as if ready to attack. Anita nervously eyed the customers watching the exchange and moved closer to him. "Oscar, watch your words. People are looking," Anita said in a hushed voice.

Oscar shrugged away from his wife's hand and stormed off toward the back of his café. Anita looked at Hannah helplessly. Hannah turned to see Colin and Chris still standing, watching them. She walked over to hear Chris's side of the story. "What happened there?" she asked him.

"You tell me," Chris replied, still fuming.

"Yesterday, Colin and I went to speak with Burke and Lucille... I believe you know them both?" Hannah asked.

Chris nodded.

"They had some interesting things to say."

Chris arched a single eyebrow. "Oh, yeah? Like what? Like I sold them a few recipes for a great deal, fair and square?"

Hannah had been hoping that her provocative, open-ended statement would lead Chris into a confession. She tried another approach. "It might be wiser for you to throw in the towel and stop stirring up so much trouble. You've got your money now, maybe you should quit while you're ahead."

Chris studied Hannah's face for a second as if evaluating her. She thought for a moment that he would agree with her and throw in the towel. Then he slid his hands into his pockets and leaned casually against the wall. "Stop stirring up trouble, huh?" he sneered. "I'm going to get what I'm owed. And no one, especially not a small town P.I., is going to tell me what to do," he said, staring her down.

Hannah felt shocked and tried not to show it.

Colin looked over at her. "All right, Chris. Time to head out of here."

Chris walked away wordlessly, casting a dirty look back at Hannah on his way out.

"What in the world just happened there?" Hannah asked Colin.

"I guess he isn't going to back down as easily as we thought," he said.

"Let's circle back with Oscar and Anita," she said.

Hannah, Colin, and Mazie walked around the outside of the store to the back entrance, hoping to avoid drawing attention to themselves and the situation. When they arrived, they saw Oscar and Anita outside, the chill of their breath suspended between their close conversation.

"Hey, you two," Hannah called feeling the need to give them a warning. "That was pretty intense, right?"

Anita and Oscar stopped their whispered conversation to look at Hannah. "Now do you see what we mean about that guy?" Anita asked.

"He's no shrinking wallflower," Hannah agreed. "Colin and I went to talk with Lucille and Burke last night, and we wanted to chat with you about what they said."

"Please, fill us in," Anita replied.

Hannah and Colin relayed the conversations they had with the other café owners. When they got to the part about Burke, Hannah noticed Oscar begin shifting from left to right as he listened.

"I was wondering why Burke would say that you two took advantage of Chris?" Hannah asked. "And what he could be talking about when he mentioned illicit activities? It doesn't sound like you at all, where could that have come from?" Hannah furrowed her brows.

"Burke is a rival who will do anything to steal our business for his own bottom line," Anita jumped in. "Right, Oscar?"

Oscar was studying a weed poking up from the concrete.

Anita tried again. "Right, Oscar?"

Oscar looked at Anita, his eyes filled with regret. "Well, Anita. I actually have something to tell you."

CHAPTER FIVE

Anita stared back at Oscar so hard, Hannah was worried she would actually bore a hole through him. "What exactly do you need to tell me?" she asked.

Oscar squeezed the back of his neck and tilted it from left to right. "Well, there might be some substance to Chris' anger." He went back to staring at the little weed in the pavement.

Anita swatted his shoulder. "Might be some substance? What does that mean?"

"Well, when we were playing around with the buttered sweet potato bread, Chris was pretty involved in that process. He tried a few recipes out and came back to me with a suggestion on the recipe. He recommended that we add some honey. I was reluctant, but tried his idea, what do you know – it was perfect."

"So that's why we have honey in the recipe?" Anita asked.

Oscar nodded.

"So, you actually stole the recipe from Chris?" she clarified, anger creeping into her voice.

"I didn't steal it, Anita," his eyes flew to meet hers. "It was a collaborative effort and we were paying him."

"Yeah, okay. It was a collaborative effort, which you took full credit for. And then accused the man of stealing *your* recipe!" Anita cried.

Oscar put his hands on Anita's shoulders, trying to calm her down. "I know, it was a bit of a mistake on my part."

"So, is all of this a joke? Chris didn't steal any of our recipes after all?" Anita threw her hands in the air in disbelief.

"No! That's not it at all. Chris did help me with this one recipe, but Anita, I'm telling you. He stole all the others.

One mistake by me doesn't justify Chris stealing all of our recipes!"

Anita was quiet. "It's hard for me to believe anything you're saying right now."

Hannah glanced at Colin who grimaced. She hated seeing her friends fight like this. "Hey, you too! Maybe we can talk about this over some coffee?" Hannah suggested.

Anita and Oscar responded by turning their backs to one another.

Hannah was pained. "Guys, we can work this out," she said.

Colin placed a hand on her shoulder and pulled her toward him. "Maybe we should give them some space," he whispered.

Hannah softened under the comforting warmth of his touch. He was right, these two needed some time to work things out between them. She walked with Colin back toward the front of the store, Mazie in tow. "It might be good to take some time away from this case while Anita and Oscar sort out the details between them," he said.

Hannah sighed. "I hate to stop investigating mid-case, but you are probably right," she said.

"But we don't have to take a break from recipes altogether," he added. "I've got some of my own that I need someone to sample at the restaurant. Do you know anyone who might be interested?" he asked her, his teasing eyes sparkling.

Mazie barked at their feet.

Hannah smiled, grateful for the distraction from thinking about her friends and their quarrel. "I happen to know two someone's," she said, gesturing at Mazie.

"Perfect. Let's go to Troughton's Trough."

The three of them walked the short distance to Colin's restaurant. Since the upscale eatery didn't have morning service, they had the place to themselves. Colin strapped on an apron and busied himself in the industrial kitchen. Hannah and Mazie sat at a stool opposite the sleek stainless-steel equipment and watched Colin work. He heated pans, sautéed butter, and boiled water with the precision of someone in a cooking competition.

It wasn't long before the whole space was filled with the smell of garlic, roasted chicken, and oak-plank salmon.

"Mmmmm," Hannah said, sniffing the air. Beside her Mazie's snout lifted. She got to her feet to follow the aroma. Colin laughed when he saw her trot over to him and quickly kicked the door to the kitchen closed. "No animals in the kitchen, I'm afraid!"

Hannah and Colin could still talk through the open bar area and just when her stomach started to rumble, he placed a beautifully plated dinner in front of her. "Voila," he said with a flourish. "Presenting my prototype recipes for next week's dinner. Please sample and give me your honest feedback."

He wiped his hands on his apron and leaned back, crossing his arms over his chest. "Oh!" he said as if something had just popped into his mind. "I forgot one thing." He reached to a plastic bowl he had filled with chopped chicken and salmon. "For Mazie," he said, placing it on the bar.

"Aww. That's so thoughtful!" she said, lowering the bowl to the ground. Mazie ran over, and in a flash had gobbled all of the pieces up. Hannah looked at Colin and grinned. "Looks like there are no complaints about the recipe so far!"

Hannah's mouth watered looking at the salmon and chicken. Beside them were garlic butter noodles and roasted broccoli. She cut into the salmon first and took a bite. She felt pressure from Colin's intense watchful eye. She closed hers and let the flood of flavors explode in her mouth. "Oh, my, gosh. This is incredible!" she said, looking at Colin.

"Really?"

"No question about it. This will be a huge hit next week," she said. "But I'd hide the recipes. I hear there is a thief on the loose."

Colin laughed. "You don't have to worry. I keep them safely locked up in here," he said, tapping the side of his temple.

"You know, I don't know how you do it," she said. "This is a real talent. And to think, I thought you were just some big investor from the city when I first met you."

Colin put his hands up. "What can I say, I'm a man of many talents," he said. His dark hair brought out his green eyes under the kitchen lights.

"Well, I've completed a thorough investigation and have determined that your business is bound to be a success!" she said, smiling at him.

Colin rounded the bar and came to sit beside Hannah. He swiveled on the stool to face her. "I have you to thank, Hannah. You were the one who gave me the courage to take my life in a new direction and encourage me to follow my dreams." He was looking intently at her.

She lowered her fork and swiveled to face him. "And I'm so glad I did. Especially if it means I can take any credit for this deliciousness." She tapped his knee and shoved it so that the stool spun him in one full circle, ending the turn by facing her again. "And while we are sharing credit. I wouldn't be a certified P.I. if it weren't for you."

"I guess we have each other to thank, then!" Colin said.

"We make a pretty good team," Hannah said, shyly, turning back to face her meal. Before Colin had a chance to respond, Hannah rushed to fill the space with words. "But I'm not feeling fully resolved about the Gomez case."

Colin chuckled. "Do tell."

"If Oscar was really involved in something underhanded, why would he come to me in the first place?"

"That's a great question," Colin replied.

"And if he *is* involved in something sinister, do I really want to be the one to crack the case? Maybe I should pull out of it," she said.

"That's an even better question. But it's one only you can answer," he said. "And I think –" Colin was interrupted by the ring of Hannah's phone.

"Excuse me, one moment," she said, placing her hand on Colin's arm. She looked to see who was calling. "It's Kate Carver," she said, wondering what the Blairstown sheriff could want.

"Hi, Kate," she answered, putting the phone on speaker so Colin could listen in.

"Hannah, I'm glad you picked up. We have an emergency."

"What is it?" Hannah asked, her worried eyes meeting Colin's as they waited for the news.

"I'm standing in front of Jolt of Java right now at a crime scene."

"Jolt of Java?" Hannah asked. She stood up and picked up her purse, already planning to head over.

"A person has just been found dead," Kate said.

Hannah gasped and moved closer to Colin.

"He's been identified as Chris Welsh."

Hannah felt weak and yet somehow relieved. She leaned into Colin who had wrapped his arms around her. "No!" she gasped. "Colin and I are heading right over," she said, hanging up the phone.

She looked at Colin, words forming in her mouth. He shook his head. "Don't say anything yet. We need to get to the crime scene to find out more details before we jump to any conclusions."

Hannah was grateful he interrupted her before she could say what she had been thinking. She had to find out where Oscar and Anita had been during the murder.

CHAPTER SIX

Colin quickly locked up Troughton's Trough, leaving the dishes unwashed, and the three of them all but ran back to the Jolt of Java. They could see the spinning blue and red lights from the patrol car down the block. When they arrived, Hannah went directly to her friend, Kate.

"Hannah, thanks for coming," she said. "Come over here with me and Ralph."

"Hi, Hannah," Ralph, Kate's loyal and stocky deputy said.

"Hi, Ralph, we meet again," Hannah said.

Kate launched in, all business. "Here's what we know. Chris was strangled. It must have happened not long ago because we have eyewitnesses that Chris was seen here, alive," she narrowed her eyes at Hannah, "and arguing with Oscar today."

Hannah flinched. "This happened in broad daylight?"

"Yes, but it was at the back of the store, where the view is mostly obstructed."

Hannah fiddled with Mazie's leash.

Kate continued. "We haven't found any fingerprints, so the killer must have worn gloves. But there is some evidence. There were traces of flour near the dead body."

Hannah twisted her face. "Oh, no."

Kate looked at her knowingly. "So, you know where this is headed, then. Oscar was found baking inside when the business next door spotted the body. And given the fact that he was seen only minutes earlier quarreling with Chris, I'm afraid he's our prime suspect," Kate finished.

Hannah let her head fall back, squeezing her eyes shut. This couldn't be happening to one of her best friends. Oscar wasn't capable of this, was he?

"I know he's your friend, Hannah. But we have to keep a neutral viewpoint during an investigation," Kate cautioned.

Hannah tilted her head up to face Kate. "I know, you're right. It's just really hard for me to imagine Oscar as a killer."

Anita, who had been in the store answering questions from the police burst out the back door. "Hannah! Oscar didn't do this! You know him! He isn't capable of murder!" she screamed.

Hannah moved toward her friend, eyeing Kate as she did. She wrapped Anita in a big hug. "Don't worry, Anita. We'll sort through all of this at the police station. I'll be with you every step of the way."

Anita began sobbing and pulled away from Hannah. "Hannah, you have to help me. Help us!" she said. "We've been friends for so long, I can't even count the years. You can't let them take Oscar!"

"Mrs. Gomez, you'll need to come with us," Ralph's voice cut through their conversation.

"Hannah – please," Anita pleaded.

"I'll take care of it. I promise," Hannah said to Anita as Ralph lead her away.

Hannah slumped down on a crate the Jolt of Java employees used for their breaks and buried her head in her hands. "Colin, what do I do?" she asked.

Mazie sensed how upset Hannah was and went to sit beside her, nuzzling her head into Hannah's leg.

"This morning I was sure you should take a break from the case," Colin said. "But with this development, I'm thinking maybe you should pick the investigation back up."

Hannah was one step ahead of him. "Here's what I can't figure out... even if Oscar stole the recipe from Chris, I can't imagine he would have taken Chris's life for it. Even after he was upset with him. Oscar isn't a violent man. He stands up for himself, as you saw, but he's never been in a physical fight since I've known him."

Colin took a seat next to Hannah, waiting for more.

"I'm wondering if Emma might have something to do with it."

"How so?" Colin asked.

"She and Chris obviously had a strained sort of relationship. And if our previous theory is correct, our suspicions that Emma was the one who convinced Christ to steal and sell the recipes, then maybe she picked this opportunity to get rid of him. For good. That way she could deflect the blame to Oscar and get away with it." Hannah was sitting up straight now, invigorated by the possibility that she could help free her friend.

"You could be right," Colin said. "We haven't spoken to Emma since you found out about her money troubles, though. Maybe we should pay her another visit?"

Hannah stood up. "That's a great idea. Plus, I need some way to help get rid of all of this adrenaline. I feel shaky and just all..." She shook out her hands as if trying to shake it off. "Should we go for a walk?"

Colin looked weary. "They live all the way across town. You sure you're up for the distance?"

Hannah nodded. "I've never been surer." She stared ahead determinedly.

Colin looked down at Mazie. "And you're sure she's up for it?"

Hannah looked at Mazie, whose tail was wagging back and forth. She looked up at Hannah and Colin as if she'd been born for the moment.

"Looks like a yes to me," Hannah said, laughing.

"I'll pop into the café and grab her something to nibble on, in case she gets hungry," Colin said.

Hannah elbowed his ribs. "In case *she* gets hungry?" she teased.

Colin smiled. "The chef didn't sample the food today, he's a little famished," he grinned.

When he emerged back outside from the Jolt of Java, pockets bursting with various pastries, the three of them were on their way to the home of the late Chris Welsh, hoping to speak with Emma.

CHAPTER SEVEN

Despite the distance from Jolt of Java to Chris's condo, they made good time with conversation, adrenaline, and pastries pushing them on. Soon, they were at the door. Hannah took a deep breath and knocked.

They waited patiently and when no one answered after a full minute, Hannah tried again, this time ringing the doorbell. They heard footsteps approach from behind the door, and then it swung open. Emma stood on the threshold of the condo, her red hair disheveled and mascara smeared down her cheek. When she saw who was there, her face took on a look of surprise. "Hannah? Colin? What are you two doing here?"

"Hi, Emma. We came to see how you're doing. You must be shocked after hearing the tragic news," Hannah said.

Emma wiped her cheek and glared at them. "I don't know how to feel. I'm in complete shock. Chris and I just broke up, and I'm currently packing my bags to move out. I was in the middle of doing so when Kate Carver called me with the news that Chris had been murdered." Her voice caught in a sob at the end of her sentence.

"Packing?" Hannah asked. She looked at Colin and raised her eyebrows when Emma looked away. "When did the two of you break up? We were just here yesterday and you both seemed really happy."

Emma calmed her jagged breaths narrowed her eyes at Hannah. "Remind me what you are doing here?"

Colin placed a hand on Hannah's back. "We want to be sure you're okay. Considering we were here yesterday visiting with you both, we're as shocked as you must be, and wanted to check on you."

Emma softened and wiped a tear that rolled down her face. "I'm doing terribly. And I'm feeling guilty about the fight we got into yesterday. I can't believe the last words I said to him were 'I never want to see you again'," she said.

"What was the fight about?" Colin asked gently.

She hardened her look at Hannah. "After you came around here asking all of your nosy questions, we got into a fight about the recipes. He had the nerve to tell me that he was going to get his payday, but he wasn't going to give me a penny. After everything I've done for him, he wasn't going to give me a red cent!" she said. Tears dry now as anger took over from sorrow, she said, "Then he broke up with me. I was so angry, I told him I never wanted to see him again... he rushed out... and now I really am never going to see him again!"

"So, after he left last night, he didn't come back?" Colin asked.

"He did come back, but he slept on the couch. I stayed in our room until I heard the front door close this morning. Then I started packing my bags.

Hannah looked thoughtful and cast a glance behind Emma at the haphazard bags stuffed with unorganized belongings. "It seems awfully convenient that the minute you knew Chris wasn't going to benefit you financially, that the two of you broke up. And even more convenient that he was found murdered not long after that. No one else saw you here, alone, did they?" she asked Emma boldly.

Emma's eyes went wide. "What are you insinuating?"

"I just think the police would want you to stay in town a little while longer. Maybe you should stop packing your bags," Hannah said.

Emma darted her glance at Hannah and then Colin. Without further warning, she used all her might to push past them both, attempting to make a run for it.

Colin instinctively reached out to grab her, when Emma responded by kicking him hard in his knee. He screamed and buckled to the ground, grabbing at his knee in pain.

Hannah ran over to Colin. "Are you okay?" she asked, crouching beside him.

"Leave me, I'll be fine. Go after Emma!" he said.

She looked at him, unsure if he meant it, but he waved her away from his position crouched on his side, clutching his knee on the floor.

Hannah stood, ready to pursue Emma when she heard the sound of a muffled scream.

"Ouch! Get this mangy mutt off of me!" Emma yelled.

Hannah ran out the front door to see Emma on the ground. Mazie was poised above her head, relentlessly licking every inch of her face. When Hannah came near, she could see that Emma was struggling to catch her breath between all of the licks.

Then Hannah felt a buzz in her pocket. She reached in to see who had called. It was Kate with a text that said she was on her way – Colin had called them for back up from his position on the floor.

Hannah sighed in relief, letting Mazie continue her lick-fest since it was keeping Emma incapacitated. She steadied her own breath as she waited beside the two of them until she saw Kate and Ralph drive toward them in their patrol car.

Ralph jockeyed his way out of the car first, while Kate angled it to ensure Emma couldn't run any further once Mazie let up.

"Emma Porter, you are coming with us," Ralph said, reaching down to cuff her hands behind her back. "We want to ask you a few questions down at the station." He hoisted her up to standing.

Emma tried to wipe her wet face on her shoulder and was still sputtering. She looked back at Hannah. "You cause trouble wherever you go!" she yelled as Ralph marched her to the car.

Satisfied that Emma was secure in police custody, Hannah walked back to the condo to check on Colin. He was sitting up now, rubbing his knee and feeding Mazie bits of croissant.

"How are you doing?" she asked him.

He reached one hand to Hannah and secured the other on the wall, struggling to his feet. "Much better now that you're here," he replied. She placed his arm over her shoulder and encouraged him to lean on her body as he hobbled his way out to the driveway.

With the patrol car heading back to the station, they both stared at the now empty driveway. She looked up at him and asked, "Do you think you are up for the distance?"

Colin hung his head and groaned, thinking about hobbling the long way back to the other side of town.

CHAPTER EIGHT

Colin collapsed on the bench in front of the precinct. "At least the station wasn't quite as far as your place," he said.

"Rest and elevate your leg, I'll grab an icepack," Hannah said. "But first I'm going in to see if Kate will let me speak with Emma. Did you want to join me?"

Colin shook his head. "I'm fine, right out here. I just need a minute off my feet."

"That seems like a good idea. Do you mind taking Mazie while I go inside?" she asked.

Colin held his hand out for her to place the leash in it. "Do your thing, Hannah," he said, wearily.

Hannah walked into the precinct and Kate saw her immediately. "Come right over, Hannah!" she gestured for her to come through the secure doors. Hannah followed Kate to her office and took a seat across from her at her desk.

"What are your thoughts about Emma?" Hannah asked.

"She seems suspicious. I didn't like how she was packing her bags and trying to get out of town. I don't like her attitude, and how little regard she seems to have for the death of her recent lover. However, she seems to have a valid alibi," Kate said.

Hannah leaned in closer. "You don't say? Where was she?"

"She told us she was at Shooters during the time Chris was murdered."

"Shooters? As in, the bar?" Hannah asked. "In the morning?"

"Yes, but evidently Shooters serves breakfast, so it's not as odd as it sounds," Kate said.

"Did anyone see her there?" Hannah asked.

"Plenty of folks did, so, unfortunately, she's no longer a suspect. She was nowhere near Jolt of Java at all today, and she went home right after her breakfast at Shooters," Kate said.

"If that's the case, why didn't she just tell that to us when we were asking her questions this morning?" Hannah asked.

"That I can't tell you, Hannah. The woman is odd, and her behavior doesn't line up for someone who just lost their boyfriend, but those aren't things we have time to investigate right now. Who knows, maybe the lenders for her business are coming after her. Since she no longer has a potential money source in Chris, she is trying to make a run for it?" Kate said.

Hannah nodded. "Maybe so. You are right, though, we don't have time to look into all of that. Who does that leave as our suspects?"

Kate looked pained and lowered her voice. "I'm so sorry, Hannah, but it seems that Oscar is our most likely suspect at this stage of the investigation."

"Kate, that can't be the case. I know he's my good friend and I'm supposed to keep my feelings and bias out of it, but in this case, that's impossible. I know him so well –

well enough to be confident of the fact that there is no way he could murder someone!"

Kate shrugged. "I hate to say it, Hannah, but that's not enough for me to go on. When you are in this business for long enough, you'll be surprised at the number of people you thought you knew."

Just then, Colin came hobbling into Kate's office, Mazie in tow. Kate looked alarmed. "Colin! What happened to you?"

"Just a little hazard in the job of a sidekick," he smiled. "I was getting bored out there, nursing my wound. I want in on the action."

"Perfect timing," Hannah said. "Oscar is currently the number one suspect. Your friend, Emma, has an alibi for the murder."

"Wait, so I have a swollen knee for nothing?" Colin said in mock disgust.

"We honor your bravery." Kate smiled.

Hannah was anxious to get back to the business of exonerating her friend. "We have to think back to the murder scene. You said you found flour there? Well, *if* Oscar did murder Chris, he's much too thoughtful a man to have left such an obvious clue behind." Hannah looked at Kate expectantly. "And why didn't he try to hide the body?"

"That's great, Hannah, but again, not enough for me to go on."

"That's a great point, actually," Colin said. "Oscar is meticulous in everything he does. What do you think about Burke Dornan? He could be a suspect. Plus, he had flour all over his store when we visited."

Hannah stood up. "That's what I was going to say. Come on, let's pay him a visit."

Colin groaned and patted his knee. "I'm not sure I'm up for much more walking today."

Kate stood up. "I'll drive you all to Hannah's car. It's the least I can do for helping to eliminate one of our suspects."

Kate dropped the three of them off at Hannah's house and waved goodbye. Then they hopped into her car and made their way over to Dornan's Desserts. They arrived at a darkened store with no one in it. The sign on the door was flipped to say "Open", but no one seemed to be working. After knocking on the front door numerous times Hannah pressed her face against the window, peaking in. "There's no sign of anyone in there," she said.

"It's very strange for a bakery to be closed in the morning. These are prime business hours for them," Colin said. "Let's go around back to see if anyone is there. Maybe they are on break."

"Unlikely, but let's take a look," Hannah said.

They walked to the back of the building and no one was there, either. Hannah tried the back door. The knob was loose, turning slightly, but the flimsy door caught by the bolt above it. "Ugh, no luck," she sighed.

Mazie sniffed the base of the door frame furiously. She was so focused on the smell; her tail was still.

"She must be smelling that sweet potato bread," Colin said.

Mazie zeroed in on the corner of the door where there was a bigger gap to stick her nose through. Then, her nose got the best of her and she aggressively nudged her face into the corner, bending the plyboard corner to wiggle her way through.

"Mazie!" Hannah called.

"I wish she could unlock it for us," Colin said.

"Mazie! Come back!" The only window at the back of the store was about eight feet up. Hannah lifted a leg up on the railing against the building and hoisted herself up. "Spot me!" she said to Colin.

She cupped her hands to her eyes and pressed against the glass, trying to see past the grime on the window. When her eyes had focused in the dark, she let out a piercing scream and released her hands. The action set her off-balance and she fell back into Colin's outstretched arms. He held her for a moment, but his knee injury caused his leg to buckle under her unexpected fall and he collapsed against the railing Hannah had just scaled.

Hannah slid out of Colin's arms, grasping the rail in an attempt to steady them both. When she was back on her feet, her breath was harried and her whole body shook.

"Are you okay?" Colin asked.

"No!" she gasped. "There's a body lying dead in there!"

CHAPTER NINE

Colin looked up at the window wishing he could climb the railing to glimpse what Hannah had just seen. "Are you sure?" he asked.

"I'm positive. I've seen enough dead bodies recently to know that he wasn't just taking a nap."

"Could you tell who it was?" he asked.

"I can't say for sure. Let's call Kate. And quickly," she shivered.

Colin took out his phone to dial Kate and Ralph. Within minutes, their familiar patrol car had pulled up to the storefront of Dornan's Desserts, lights flashing.

"Watch out for Mazie," Hannah called.

Ralph nodded and wasted no time kicking down the front door. A trail of three other police officers followed behind him, guns drawn.

"I didn't even think of the fact that the murderer could still be in there with the body," Hannah said to Colin, shivering and leaning closer to him. They watched the officers charge through the front door, announcing their presence and looking in dark corners for anyone hiding.

Colin put his arm around Hannah. "I wonder how Mazie's doing in there. Either she's terrified, or she's in a sweet potato bread food coma," Colin said.

Once the officers had cleared the scene and declared no imminent danger, Hannah and Colin stepped into the store, careful to walk around the broken glass from the shattered front door.

They went to the back where Hannah had seen the body. When they were close enough to see it in person, Hannah and Colin stopped to study it. "It was Burke," Hannah confirmed.

"Poor guy. He's sure seen better days," Colin said.

"On the other hand, it looks like Mazie is doing just fine," Hannah said, pointing to the beagle, who sat proudly beside Burke's body as if to protect him. But beside the pup, were crumbs of sweet potato bread, indicating that guarding the body was not all she'd been doing in the store. "You little rascal," Hannah said, bending to scoop the dog into her arms.

Kate looked over at Mazie and Hannah. "Find any clues there, little pup?"

Hannah scratched behind Mazie's ears and smiled. "Beagles search with their noses, but they always follow their stomachs!" she said to Kate.

Hannah and Colin left the dead body to walk around the rest of the small dessert shop, trying to find any other clues. There were no footprints and no trace of anyone else having been in the shop. "Who else has access to the store?" Hannah asked.

"Maybe Burke's employees?" Colin suggested. "However, Burke seems like the kind of guy who doesn't like to relinquish control, so I'm not confident anyone would have a key to get in. They'd have to be someone who was already here."

"And since there was no sign of a forced entry, it must have been someone Burke knows well and didn't have suspicions about letting in," Hanna added.

They circled back to the body, hoping that Ralph had found more clues on the body itself.

Hannah stood behind the yellow crime scene tape and surveyed the working officers. "Any other clues on Burke's body?" she asked.

Ralph walked toward Hannah. "Based on his body temperature, we know that Burke has been dead longer than Chris has. So, he was murdered before Chris at some point this morning."

Hannah's eyes lit up. "How *much* longer?" she asked.

Ralph scratched his chin. "Hmm, it's hard to say exactly without an autopsy, but I'm thinking he's been gone since at least 6:00 A.M. this morning," he said. Then he furrowed his brows and stared at Burke's body as if deep in thought. "I wonder where Emma was this morning when Burke was murdered," he said, looking at Kate.

"I'm wondering if we should rethink her whole story. Considering when Chris's body was found today, we'll need to take another look at Emma's alibi. I knew there was something fishy about her behavior," Kate said.

Hannah and Colin stepped away from the caution tape, still carrying Mazie. She looked toward Colin. "The good news is that this most likely exonerates Oscar," she said.

"How do you mean?" Colin asked.

"Oscar may not have had an alibi when Chris was murdered, but at 6:00 A.M. I'm sure Anita was with him and can vouch for the fact that he wasn't Burke's killer. It seems to me that these killings had to be done by the same person. So, if Oscar didn't kill Burke, he didn't kill Chris," she said.

"Well, that's a relief," Colin said. "I hate that this sort of situation makes me doubt people."

"I know," Hannah agreed. "The problem is that since he's been accused of the crime already, his reputation has been sullied. I hope folks in the community won't look at him any differently now."

"Time will take care of that," Colin said. "Especially when you find the real killer. They will be so busy discussing it, they'll forget all about Oscar."

Hannah snuggled the dog a little bit closer, rubbing her cheek against Mazie's. "I'm hopeful you are right about that," she said.

"You'll see," Colin smiled reassuringly.

Hannah squared her shoulders. "All right, back to the business of finding Chris' killer. Burke is dead, so he's no longer a suspect. Emma has an alibi. Oscar is no longer in the line of fire. That only leaves one suspect."

Colin looked at her expectantly, waiting for her to reveal the name.

CHAPTER TEN

"Follow me," she said.

Colin didn't move and put his hands on his hips. "I need the name!" he said.

Hannah, already a few paces ahead, turned back to look at him. She threw her hands up as if he should have read her mind. "We're going to Cody's Café!" she cried and headed toward the car.

Colin nodded his head in realization. "Ah, Lucille Cody!" he recalled, hobbling after Hannah as fast as his knee would allow him.

The three of them settled into the car, Mazie on Colin's lap, as Hannah started the engine. She looked at the passenger's seat. "All set?"

"All set!" he replied. Mazie even let out a little bark, as her head darted around, wondering where she was being taken now.

Hannah reversed with the precision of a race car driver, narrowly avoiding the cars parked beside her.

"Wow, Hannah. I haven't seen you drive like this before," Colin noted.

"That's because you are always driving," she replied with a sly smile. "It also helps that I'm very motivated to pay Lucille a visit," she added.

"Thanks for not making me hobble my way over there. I'm hoping this knee heals sooner rather than later," he said, gently rubbing his still swollen injury.

"Of course," Hannah replied. "Plus, this way we get there faster," she winked teasingly in his direction.

They were there in no time and now that it was mid-morning, traffic at the bakery had died down. Hannah watched as a line of people piled out of the store. "Looks like we got here right after rush hour," she said. She walked around to the other side of the car, opening Colin's door for him. "Sir," she said, offering her arm to assist in getting him out of the vehicle.

He gently shoved it away. "Nope. I can do it myself. Here, take Mazie," he said, handing Mazie's leash to her. "That will be the biggest help."

Hannah smiled, knowing he would react that way. She thought maybe it would help speed his healing process slightly if she babied him a little bit. However, she figured he'd take it as an insult to his independence. He held onto both the door frame and the door to hoist himself out of the seat. "There we go," he said, brushing his hands together. "All set." He shut the door and followed behind a grinning Hannah to the front door of Cody's Café.

Lucille stood behind the counter serving customers. She looked up when she heard the doorbells jingle. "Ah, Hannah, Colin!" she said. "To what do I owe the pleasure?"

Hannah walked into the café with Mazie on a leash. They happened to hit a lull in customers, as no one else was in the store. "We just swung by to ask you a few questions," Hannah said. "I'm not sure if you've heard the most recent news?" she asked her.

Lucille's face darkened. "I was so sorry to hear about Oscar's arrest. I know you were good friends with him. I really hope everything works out as it should." She crouched low to rearrange some pastries in the glass display.

"Thank you so much, Lucille," Hannah said. "I'm just so worried about Oscar. I don't think he did it, but I'm afraid the evidence is stacked against him. I hope he can find a way to prove his innocence, but it's not looking good." Hannah said, concern clouding her face.

Colin gave her a side glance and Hannah returned a look to him, a look that said, "I'll explain later!"

"I just don't know if Oscar can work his way out of the mess, he's gotten himself into," she finished, watching to see Lucille's reaction.

Lucille stayed focused on stacking and restacking the croissants in her display case. She didn't respond.

Hannah tried another approach. She lowered her voice and added, "If Oscar does ultimately get arrested for the murder, with Chris dead, no one else is left to benefit from the telltale recipes." This time, she saw Lucille's arm flinch in the display case. "That will serve you well, right? No one else has access to them, and the whole town will come to your café to get their favorite pastries?"

Lucille stood up to straighten her apron. Hannah watched as a puff of flour came off of it as she did so. Then she noticed a streak of flour on the arm of Lucille's black shirt. "I suppose you may be right about that," Lucille said. "But given that I did buy the recipe at a fair price, it would only seem prudent that I'd profit from them eventually. Although, it would be a pity to gain business at the expense of others' misfortune," she was careful to add.

Hannah was fully convinced of her suspicions now. She took a step toward the woman, placing her hands on the glass counter. "I have another idea of who may have killed Chris," she said.

Lucille slowly turned to look at Hannah, eyeing her hands on the glass counter. "Oh? And what is that idea, if I may ask?" she said in a measured tone.

Hannah straightened her back and took a big intake of breath. "I think you killed Chris, hoping to frame Oscar for the crime. I guess Burke just got in your way, his business may have challenged yours by using the recipes Chris sold you. You had to kill him and as you were already planning to kill Chris... well I guess Burke didn't matter either," she stood with her arms at her hips watching Lucille. Next to her, Colin let out a low whistle.

Lucille laughed mockingly. "Well now, that really is *quite* the hypothesis," she said.

"It is... and now, you are the only one left to reap the profits from the stolen recipes. With all three of you baking the same potato bread, the market in this town was saturated. People could go down the road to get the same treat. But now that you've taken out your two biggest rivals, all the profit is yours. Isn't that right?" Hannah asked.

Lucille held Hannah's eye contact. She laughed again, but her smile didn't quite reach her eyes. "That's a stretch, Hannah," she said casually.

Mazie had been sniffing the air during the exchange, and she suddenly bolted towards the kitchen, ripping her leash out of Colin's hand. "Oh, no! Sorry about that!" Colin said.

"No problem, you and your knee stay here, I'll be right back!" Hannah followed after her, rushing through the swinging door to find Mazie on her hind legs, reaching her front paws up to lean on the counter, sniffing the air. Hannah could see what she was smelling. There was nothing but sweet potato bread, as far as the eye could see. Rows upon rows of the treat covered every surface of the kitchen.

Lucille wasn't far behind and came shuffling into the kitchen after them.

"Sorry about that," Hannah said to Lucille. "Sometimes her nose has a mind of its own."

Lucille attempted a smile. "Well, let's get the animal out of the kitchen then, shall we?" she said gesturing to the door.

"Of course," Hannah replied. "However, I did want to finish by giving you the courtesy of telling you that I'm going to call my friend, Kate, the police chief, and have her question you at the police station." Hannah saw Lucille's shoulders slump and she walked toward Mazie and lifted her up. When she turned around to leave the kitchen, she saw Lucille reach into the sink for a stray frying pan and before she knew it, the woman was charging directly at her!

CHAPTER ELEVEN

"There will be no going to the precinct for questioning!" Lucille said as she charged toward Hannah, frying pan suspended behind her head.

Hannah froze on the spot and didn't have much time to react. She instinctively lowered Mazie back to the floor to protect the dog from the rogue pan. When she was crouched lower to the floor, she had an idea. She would stay low and tackle Lucille's legs.

Lucille seemed to see the move coming, and lowered the frying pan, readying it to hit Hannah in her crouched position. She wound it up behind her, as if she was at the batting cages, and took a big swing.

Hannah saw it coming and managed to maneuver out of the way, just in time. The frying pan came to a clanging stop when it hit the oven, instead of Hannah's head. The vibration down the handle reverberated in Lucille's grip and she dropped the pan, shaking her hand. "Ugh, never mind!" she said. Then, she crouched low to match Hannah's stance. They circled one another as if they were in a wrestling match. Hannah couldn't help but be impressed at the surprising agility of the older, plumper woman.

Lucille took advantage of her split second of distraction and charged, slamming her left shoulder into Hannah's stomach. Hannah fell back with a painful splat, landing on her back on the kitchen floor. Lucille kept her arms pinned to the floor with her knees, stilling all of Hannah's efforts to resist the powerful woman.

"Let me go!" Hannah shouted. She wriggled with all of her might to be free, but Lucille's grip was too strong.

"Not a chance. I paid good money for those recipes, and I alone will reap the profits, just as soon as all of my competitors are out of the way!" Then she looked down at Hannah giving her an evil stare. "And, all of my detractors."

Mazie had been startled out of her senses when Hannah

had let her down. She scampered out of the way when she saw Lucille barreling toward them, her instinct kicking in. Now she saw her owner in peril and ran back and forth beside Hannah who was rendered incapacitated by Lucille. Mazie sensed that it wasn't a playfight and started jumping at the back of Lucille. With every jump up, she nipped Lucille's hair, pulling at it slightly.

"Ouch, get off of me, dog!" Lucille yelled, but she couldn't risk shooing the animal away, lest it gave Hannah an advantage to break free.

"Get her, Mazie!" Hannah yelled, causing Lucille to grip her arms tighter.

Mazie jumped more frantically, now nipping at Lucille's hair and back. On one jump, she reached for Lucille's upper arm and finally managed to get a bigger chunk of skin in her teeth, causing Lucille to scream and grab the spot Mazie was growling and clinging to.

Hannah took the opportunity to shove Lucille off of her and was able to scramble to her feet, grabbing in the nearest drawer for some sort of weapon. She reached in and withdrew a spatula. She looked at the floppy black plastic tip and slumped slightly.

Lucille rolled off of Hannah and shook Mazie away. She sat up to see Hannah brandishing the sorry looking weapon. "Ha!" she scoffed. "A lot of good that will do you!" She stood up and inched along the countertops to the place she knew the knives would be. She opened the drawer, the sound of silverware clanging together as she felt around. "One more murder from me will be nothing," she glared at Hannah.

Since Lucille shoved Mazie off of her, she had been following the woman, growling. Now she bared her teeth and attacked her knee viciously. Lucille let go of her grip on the knife and collapsed to the floor. "You mangey mutt!" she cried.

Hannah took the opportunity to move toward Lucille, attempting to subdue the woman, when Kate and Ralph burst into the kitchen, guns drawn.

Hannah looked toward them and slumped onto the counter, relief washing over her. "I thought you'd never get here!" she cried.

Colin limped in behind them, eyes wide and on Hannah. "I'm so sorry I wasn't here sooner," he said, making his way over to her.

She collapsed into his arms. "You're here now," she said, leaning into his chest.

Kate marched toward Lucille. "You are under arrest. Anything you say can and will be used against you in the court of law," she said, reading Lucille her Miranda Rights.

Lucille tried to jerk her body away from Kate. "Ralph! A little assistance here?" Kate called to her partner. Ralph came over to hold Lucille steady as Kate successfully cuffed her.

"You have no proof that I did anything!" she yelled. "You can't arrest someone just because you are suspicious! Or because you are a terrible P.I.!" she said, looking directly at Hannah.

Hannah lifted her head from Colin's chest tiredly. "You're right, Lucille. You can't arrest someone on suspicion alone. Which is why I'm wearing a wire and recorded you confessing to the murder of both Chris Welsh and Burke Dornan," she said.

Colin held her away and looked at her, shocked. "Nice work on that one!" he said.

Hannah's surprise announcement silenced Lucille. She dropped her head and slouched forward, allowing Ralph and Kate to take her away with no further fight. Hannah let out a deep exhale as she watched her escorted out of the kitchen.

"What about you, you okay down there?" Hannah asked Mazie. "You saw a lot of action today for an ex-police dog," she joked, referencing Mazie's former career before she had to retire early due to an injury.

For her part, Mazie didn't even look up. She was too busy munching away on the sweet potato bread that had been scattered on the floor in the fight.

Hannah couldn't help but laugh.

CHAPTER TWELVE

Kate and Ralph escorted a yelling Lucille to the police station in the back of their patrol car, lights flashing all the way through town. Lucille fiercely denied any allegations or suggestions that she could be involved somehow with the double murders. This continued right up until Kate played the recording of the wire Hannah wore in the kitchen. Lucille was suddenly silent and subsequently booked and held without bail. The case was closed.

Hannah stopped by the police station that evening to check on the status of things. "Hannah, my favorite P.I.! Come on back here," Kate greeted her.

Hannah went back to Kate's office to debrief the case.

"You've been making my job significantly easier these days, Hannah. We wouldn't have been able to solve this case without you," she said.

"Anything I can do to help, Kate," she replied. "Plus, with Oscar wrongly accused, I had a little bit more skin in this particular game. Even though I know I'm supposed to keep my emotions out of it," she added with a chuckle.

Kate's eyes crinkled in a smile. "That's tough to do sometimes, isn't it? Though they don't say this in the training manual, sometimes it's great motivation to solve the case for their sake. As long as you know with certainty that they are innocent," she winked at Hannah.

"I brought a little something to celebrate the case being closed," Hannah said, reaching into a brown paper bag.

Kate's eyes perked up as she leaned over the desk for a better look.

Hannah produced two pieces of sweet potato bread and presented one to Kate with a flourish. "Behold, the treat so sweet, people would literally kill for it," she said.

Kate groaned at the joke but took a bite of the bread anyway. "Hmm, and now I can finally taste why!" she said. "That is good!"

* * *

CRIME IN BLAIRSTOWN had slowed down in the weeks following the recipe murders, and everyone seemed grateful for that. Hannah took the opportunity to spend the next few weeks settling into her office, organizing files, and making her space a place that put your mind at ease. With the help of Colin, of course, as the whole thing had been his suggestion. Her P.I. business had started so quickly and successfully, she hardly had time to take care of the office work.

Once her files and books had a place, her pictures were hung and her desk was organized, Hannah ran a vacuum over the carpet as a finishing touch. Mazie, who had been snoozing in her dog bed and happily ignoring Hannah's efforts, was suddenly wide awake with the roar of the vacuum. She jumped up and followed behind Hannah's heels, barking until she had finished her final task.

"Okay, Mazie. I'm all done now!" she said, wrapping the cord around the handle and tucking the vacuum back into the closet. Then she collapsed onto her couch and let all of the strain of her hard work fall out of her body. Mazie scrambled up beside her, licking her face.

Hannah giggled, scratching behind her ears. "What do you say we go get a treat at Jolt of Java?" she asked her pup. Mazie had heard those words enough to know what they meant. She jumped off the couch and sat by the door, right under the place her leash hung.

Hannah maneuvered herself up from the couch and clipped Mazie's leash onto her harness before heading out on the short walk to see her two good friends.

When they approached the quaint coffee shop, she saw that the tables were all full and there was even a line formed at the counter. Hannah smiled at the realization that Oscar's involvement in the scandal had passed over and people seemed to have moved on. Hannah entered the coffee shop and breathed in the familiar, comforting smell of the freshly ground coffee beans. She positioned herself at the back of the line, hoping to surprise her friends working hard behind the counter.

"What can I get for you, miss?" Oscar asked when she made it to the front of the line. He looked up from behind the register and realized who he was talking to.

"Hannah! It's on the house, my friend! Would you like an extra-large latte? Maybe a pastry?" he grinned.

"Sure, those sound great! I'm here for a treat to celebrate finally organizing my office," she said.

At the mention of the word treat, Mazie wagged her tail and let out a little yip.

"Is that Mazie down there?" Oscar asked, leaning over the counter. "Anita! Come on over here, our favorite customers have paid us a visit," he called his wife.

"Is that Hannah? Oscar, let's take a break to catch up with her a little while," she said.

Oscar motioned their employee's over so he and Anita could chat with Hannah for a little while. They removed their aprons and joined her at her favorite table by the fireplace.

"So," Hannah said, happy to be in the company of her two friends, who were not murderers. "What's new? Tell me everything!"

Oscar looked around the café. "As you can see, the business has picked back up, so we are grateful for that."

Anita nodded and placed her hand on Oscar's. "We've also made a decision to discuss every recipe with one another and to give a percentage of the profits from the sweet potato bread to Emma or Chris's family. Our lawyer is looking into it. He said we don't really need to as the bread was developed as part of Chris's employment, technically it is ours, but we just feel better this way." she said.

"We will share our recipes, and I have vowed to only focus on my own original recipes moving forward," Oscar added. "I'll only collaborate with Anita, so there is absolutely no confusion!"

"That sounds like a great decision. I'm sure you can both come up with fantastic recipes," Hannah said. She broke off a piece of the scone Oscar had given her. "Is this one of your new ones?" she asked, dropping a piece for Mazie.

"Yes, that's ours," Oscar said with pride. "What do you think?"

At that moment, the three of them heard a coughing sound from under the table. They bent to look and saw that Mazie had just spit out the piece of scone. They all lifted their heads back up to look at one another awkwardly.

"I guess we have some tweaks to make on that particular recipe," Anita said sheepishly.

"Oh, don't mind Mazie. I'm sure it's delicious!" Hannah said, the flush of embarrassment creeping up her neck. "She's picky, for a dog," she added.

Anita cast a glance back toward the line of people that had grown since Hannah arrived. "We'd better get back to help out behind the counter. We don't need another reason for people to stop coming here!" she joked.

Oscar and Anita gave Hannah a big hug. "It's always so nice to see you, Hannah. Come back again soon," Oscar said.

Hannah finished her coffee and discreetly slipped the rest of the scone into the garbage by the door. Then she led Mazie out for a little stroll around town. They took in the beautifully colored leaves that stubbornly clung to the branches trying to shake them off. There was a crisp scent in the air that only a looming winter held. She felt content. She had her puppy and her job, and she was happy.

The sound of her name jarred her out of her daydream. "Hannah!"

She turned to the familiar, deep voice and was face to face with Colin's piercing green eyes. "Hey, Colin," she said brightly. "What are you doing out of Troughton's Trough at this time of day? I know I promised you some chocolate cake but I thought you would be too busy until later."

He rubbed the back of his neck and glanced at her, almost shyly. "The chocolate cake can wait... I was actually looking for you two ladies." Mazie wagged her tail as he looked down at her.

"Is that right?" Hannah asked. "What can we do for you? Do you have a recipe for us to test or a crime for us to solve?"

Colin laughed. "This isn't work-related at all. In fact, it's exactly the opposite."

Hannah's eyes lit up and clapped her hands together. "Do tell!"

He dropped his hands into his pockets and looked at Hannah. "Will you come to Troughton's Trough?"

Hannah looked back, perplexed at his sudden serious tone. "Of course, I will! I love your restaurant."

He shook his head slightly. "No, I mean, will you come as my date?" He looked into her eyes, shifting from right foot to left.

A warmth spread through her veins. "Just so I'm clear, you are asking me on a date? With you?" Her eyes sparkled up at Colin.

He smiled and dropped his eyes. Then he reached for both of her hands to hold in his. "Yes. That's what I'm asking."

Hannah's grin spread involuntarily across her face. "Of course, I will," she said. Then Mazie, who had sensed a shift in the mood, put one paw up on Hannah's leg, and one on Colin's. She looked back and forth between them, panting.

"Oh, right! Sorry, Mazie." She peered up at Colin. "What do we do about Mazie, is she invited?"

Colin reached to pat Mazie's head. "I know by now that you two are a package deal. Mazie is more than welcome. In fact, I have a plan for her."

"Oh really?" she asked.

He reached into his pocket and withdrew something covered in aluminum foil. He gently peeled back the layers, revealing a piece of banana bread.

Hannah raised her eyebrows. "Is this an appetizer for our date?" she asked.

Colin chuckled. "No, Hannah. It's not an appetizer for us. But it might be for Mazie. I was inspired by your most recent case, and this is a new recipe we developed. It's a banana bread prepared specifically for dogs."

"I hope it's good," she said. "Mazie already rejected a pastry this morning. She won't pretend to like it."

Colin ripped off a piece of the bread.

They both looked to the beagle sitting proud and waiting patiently. Colin tossed a piece to her. They watched her, waiting.

Mazie caught it out of the air and gobbled it up in one bite. Then she sat staring at Colin, hoping for more.

"Success!" he said.

"Whew!" Hannah replied. "I guess that means we can officially move ahead with our date, then."

"I'm so glad to hear it."

"Colin, thank you for all of your help with me on my recent cases," Hannah said. "And for making Mazie special bread so you and I can have time alone. You're always so thoughtful."

Colin smiled down at Hannah, then he reached toward her, slipping his hand into hers. She felt an electric pulse fly up her arm and leaned into Colin slightly. They turned to walk down the tree-lined sidewalk toward the restaurant, with Mazie trotting along beside them.

* * *

THE BAKERS AND BULLDOGS MYSTERIES COLLECTION 20 BOOK BOX SET - PREVIEW

Ding. Melody stretched the dough a little further; holding her breath as she expertly pulled it just enough to ensure a perfectly thin, translucent layer. The bell pinged again, and Melody glanced around for Kerry.

"Hey, Ker—where are you?" she called, failing to detect her assistant's presence. Melody shook her head, wiped her hands on her apron, exited the kitchen and hurried into the shop. There stood her best customer, Alvin Hennessy, the small town's local sheriff, his kind brown eyes lighting up as Melody came into his view. He hastily removed his hat, cleared his throat and smiled sheepishly down at her.

"Oh, hey there, Mel. Sorry to stop in again today, but I forgot I needed a cake for Ma's hen party tonight." Alvin shuffled his feet shyly, his cheeks reddening.

Melody sighed. She was grateful for his business, but suspected he purposely cut his order in two so he had an excuse to drop by twice today. She would have preferred efficiency, but good manners and a genuine fondness for the sheriff prevented her from showing any exasperation. She should be flattered by his attention—she knew, but she really wasn't interested in a romantic relationship at this point in her life. Not that he wasn't handsome, in his own way, but he was just not her type, she supposed, even if she *were* in the market for a romantic relationship. She took a quick moment to evaluate his appearance. He possessed the long, lean lines of a thoroughbred, but somehow wasn't able to project his inherent attractiveness, even in uniform. Perhaps it was his constant grinning. It made him appear a little strange, no, that wasn't really it; it was more his inability to realize his own appeal, a slight insecurity, an awkwardness. She mentally shook herself and focused on the business at hand.

"Not a problem, Al. Always good to see you!" she said, forcing a smile.

She felt a pang of guilt at her fib, but knew she probably made his day with her comment. In spite of her uncanny ability to notice and discern the overt as well as hidden attributes of others, Melody possessed a baffling blindness to her own qualities. She could have easily graced the pages of any magazine, even in jeans and her trademark logoed tee. An Irish beauty, Melody was blessed with more than her fair share of pluses: glossy auburn, shoulder-length tresses (albeit piled on her head and anchored with a hairnet), an angelic face, and statuesque curves to rival any pin-up girl. She had many secret (and not so secret) male admirers in town, but even though she was consistently friendly and courteous, she possessed an intimidating blend of self-assurance, the formerly discussed unawareness of her beauty, and a steadfast personal rule against flirting.

"What kind of cake did you have in mind? We have a cream cheese-filled red velvet and an orange-hickory nut on hand. Kerry made them yesterday, and they're still fresh."

As if summoned by her name, Kerry rushed in, flinging out hyper apologies as she whipped on an apron over her uniform of sparkly blue jeans and the shop's logo-emblazoned t-shirt.

"Where were you?" Melody asked.

"I forgot my phone in my car and wanted to make sure Aunt Rita didn't call with her family reunion order. I told her to call the shop rather than my cell, but she never remembers the number and can't be bothered to look it up. Good thing I checked; as she did leave me a voicemail with what she wants, and she's hoping to get everything tomorrow afternoon, even though the reunion doesn't start until Friday evening!" Kerry's words tumbled over each other as her hands gestured wildly. Melody wondered how Kerry was able to breathe while talking at such a rate.

"I see you've gone over your quota of caffeine today," Melody teased, noting Kerry's messy blond bun slipping out of the hair net stretched crookedly over her head and the slight sheen of sweat on her brow.

Kerry, plump and pretty, was engaged to Port Warren High's beloved football coach, George Stanley, who adored her. In Kerry's mind, this gave her free reign to play matchmaker with all her unfortunately single friends and acquaintances, especially her beautiful boss.

"Yeah, might have overdone the go-juice just a tad." Kerry chuckled, tucking her stray blond strands back into the net. Kerry then turned her attention to their visitor. "Hey, Al, you forget something? Weren't you in earlier?"

Alvin blushed and nodded, looking down at his shoes and rubbing his close-cropped brown hair.

Kerry smiled wickedly at his obvious discomfiture. "I'm beginning to think this is your new office!"

Melody gave her a quick, pursed-lip glare, knowing it would only encourage her would-be marriage broker to continue to tease poor Alvin.

"Yep, completely forgot about Ma's card deal tonight; she wanted me to pick up a cake; whatcha got in stock?" Alvin asked trying to recover himself.

As the sheriff switched his embarrassed attention to his torturer, Melody took the opportunity to slip quietly back into the kitchen to finish the croissants, leaving Kerry to fill Alvin's order. She concentrated, cutting and folding thin strips into perfect crescents.

"That guy's got it bad!" Kerry announced as she sailed into the kitchen, automatically beelining it for the coffee machine.

"No! You're cut off!" Melody was quick to see her assistant's intention and she grabbed Kerry's sleeve with a floury hand, "No more coffee for you!"

Kerry sheepishly set the pot back down and crossed her arms. She eyed the tray of bakery rejects that failed Melody's perfectionistic eye, sighed, and helped herself to a broken cookie. Nibbling, she glared at Melody.

"You've got it bad," Melody insisted. "You're torturing that poor man, and you know it! What did he end up buying?"

"Don't try and change the subject! That dog is one whipped puppy. If he really forgot that cake this morning, I'm a one-eyed frog. His mom has bridge every Wednesday night, tonight is no exception!" Kerry exclaimed while munching through a second cookie reject.

Melody shrugged, not wanting to encourage that line of thinking. She'd known for a while that Alvin had a thing for her. She tried her best to ignore it and avoid him as much as possible. With her busy schedule, she just wasn't ready for anything serious, even if it was with someone like Alvin. Or was it really about her schedule? Whatever, she was just not into a relationship at the moment. She had to admit, he was a good guy. And he would probably treat her right if she ever gave him a chance. But it was just too soon.

"He's either going to have to man up and ask you out or go broke buying donuts and cakes! For a lawman, he ain't very brave!" Kerry added.

Melody let her rattle on, hoping Kerry would run out of words on the subject, though that seemed unlikely.

Kerry propped her chin on her left palm looking all dreamy. "I think he's cute, though, don't you? A little on the puppy dog side, but still pretty manly when he's not tripping over his tongue when you're around."

Melody sighed, rolled her eyes, and kept silent. It was her weapon of choice and it worked well with Kerry, whose main hobby was verbalizing, combined with taking off on frequent, caffeine-infused rabbit trails. So, Kerry prattled on while Mel took a moment to mull over the situation.

In truth, she almost wished she reciprocated Alvin's apparent feelings. She dreaded the day she would really have to reject such a nice guy. She blew out a breath of frustration, hoping against hope that he would never find the courage to approach her romantically because in that way she could avoid the whole ordeal. If he did ever find the courage to ask her out, she would just have to find a nice way to turn him down. Maybe she should start thinking about how she could get out of it without hurting his feelings.

Her thoughts, generally practical, quickly switched over to Aunt Rita's reunion and she broke into Kerry's monologue.

"Which cake did the sheriff end up buying? And what does Aunt Rita need by Friday?" Melody asked and Kerry cooperated with the subject change, her talking talent showcased by her ability to jump off and on any topic train.

"He decided on the red velvet. Auntie said she needs three cakes: one devil's food, one pineapple upside down, and one hummingbird. I think I should call her and steer her away from the hummingbird, as it's too similar to the pineapple upside-down—don't you think? Maybe a pecan Texas sheet instead? Add a little variety? Also, she wants two-dozen each of chocolate chip, short-bread and peanut butter cookies, an apple strudel and six dozen dinner rolls. I think I better tell her to freeze everything when she gets it tomorrow since she's not serving most of it until Saturday and Sunday, and I wouldn't think she'd like them anything but fresh.

Really, she should get everything from us Friday afternoon; we could have it done by two, don't you think? Maybe I should call her? Maybe not, as she never changes her mind once she makes a plan; maybe you should call her? She'd probably listen to you better than me. But maybe freezing them would be good enough and then we wouldn't be as stressed on Saturday, as we have that wedding cake to deliver and set up, and Jeannette isn't somebody we want to disappoint with shoddy work..." Kerry continued to ponder the quandary of her aunt's order while she bustled about wiping counters, putting away clean tools from the dish drainer, and checking—and double-checking—the stores of supplies.

Just then the bell dinged, heralding another customer, and Kerry whisked out of the kitchen.

Melody opened the oven and placed the croissant trays inside, setting the timer as she finished. She could hear Kerry's voice, presumably talking to a customer, and while tempted to start on tomorrow's orders, she knew she should make an appearance in the shop as some of her customers took it very personally when she was too busy to greet them.

Kerry's Aunt Rita stood at the counter, her lips pursed as she listened to her niece's flood of advice. Rita held up her hand, finally getting Kerry to slow her word flow. Aunt Rita had a closet full of old-fashioned, 50's style dresses that belted at the waist, everything from floral, to stripes and plaids, to plain. She only ever wore dark brown, laced up walking shoes, white gloves, and netted hats whenever she ventured outside her house. Inside, she wore button-up housedresses, ones she deemed suitable for the constant cleaning she inflicted on her house. Dust was terrified to land anywhere in her vicinity.

"I need everything by tomorrow afternoon, Kerry Ann, is that going to be a problem?" Just as Kerry opened her mouth to answer, Rita caught sight of Melody.

"Thank God you're here! My niece seems to think I don't know my own mind, and I need her to understand that I need everything tomorrow afternoon. I will be extremely busy with other reunion tasks... of course, I have to do everything myself, the rest of the family cannot be trusted... so I need the desserts squared away tomorrow. Is that too difficult?" Rita glared at Melody belligerently.

"Oh no, Rita, tomorrow afternoon is perfect! We don't have another big order besides yours due until Friday afternoon, so it will work out just fine, and your choices show nice forethought and variety," Melody assured her.

"Hmph. Kerry Ann here seems to think I don't have enough variety in the cake department. I keep trying to explain that Cousin Harold loves the pineapple upside down and my sister must have hummingbird. There is no room for substitutes. Now, I need to know if those choices are going to be a problem? I don't want to take my business elsewhere, but my friend Alice's cousin bakes and sells cakes out of her kitchen, so I do have other options," Rita continued to scowl pugnaciously at her niece while she directed her question to Melody.

"No, we can certainly bake all your choices," Melody replied calmly. "All your selections are just fine, and there is no finer cake baker than your niece here!"

Mollified, Kerry let go of her need to adjust Aunt Rita's cake menu, and smiled at her employer, "Awww shucks, boss-lady! You're the best!"

"Hmph," Rita grunted, clutching her giant purse more firmly to her chest, as if perhaps Melody and Kerry weren't to be trusted; she then adjusted her old-fashioned hat and exited with, "Okay then. I'll expect your delivery tomorrow afternoon, but no earlier than two pm, as I'll need an afternoon rest with all this working myself to death. And for what? Some ungrateful relatives who don't mind reaping the benefits of all my back-breaking labor!"

Kerry groaned, shaking her head. As soon as her aunt was out of earshot, she commented, "Oh my God, Aunt Rita is something else, isn't she? No wonder Uncle Leroy left this earth... her sunny disposition probably poisoned him to death!"

Melody smiled, suspecting Kerry probably inherited her aunt's opinionated personality, and ability to talk at lightspeed. Though Kerry was liberally tempered with cheerfulness, Rita lacked pretty much any positive modifying trait.

The Bakers and Bulldog Mysteries Collection – Grab all 20 books in this much loved series with the cutest French Bulldog Detective in all of Port Warren.

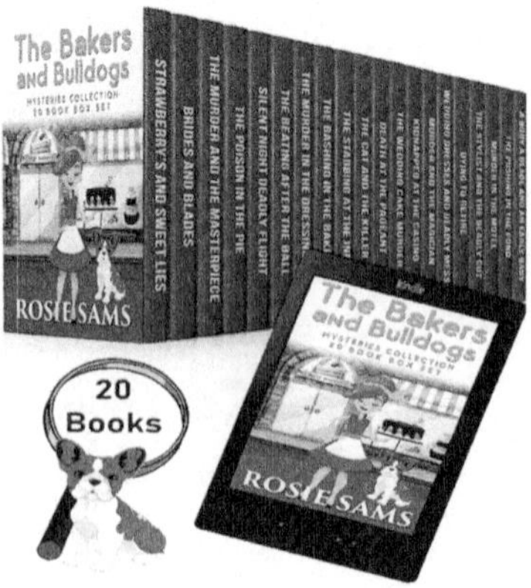

ALSO BY ROSIE SAMS & AGATHA PARKER

To be the first to find out when Rosie & Agatha release a new book and to hear about other sweet romance authors join the exclusive SweetBookHub readers club here.

* * *

The Dog Detectives – The Beagle Mysteries

The Beagle Mysteries book 1 to 6 all in this amazing value Box Set

Adding up to Murder

Murder for the Crafty Ladies and the Clever Beagle

The Stabbing of the Star

By Rosie Sams

The Art of Murder

If you enjoyed this book, Rosie and Agatha would appreciate it if you left a review on Amazon or Goodreads